The Pueblo Indians

by Pamela Ross

Consultants:
Pat Reck, Curator
Joe Sando, Historian
Indian Pueblo Cultural Center

Bridgestone Books

an imprint of Capstone Press
Mankato, Minnesota

Bridgestone Books are published by Capstone Press
151 Good Counsel Drive, P.O. Box 669, Mankato, Minnesota 56002
http://www.capstone-press.com

Library of Congress Cataloging-in-Publication Data
Ross, Pamela, 1962–
    The Pueblo Indians/by Pamela Ross.
    p. cm.—(Native peoples)
    Includes bibliographical references and index.
    Summary: Provides an overview of the past and present lives of the Pueblo
Indians, covering their daily activities, customs, family life, religion, government,
history, and interaction with the United States government.
    ISBN 0-7368-0079-4
    1. Pueblo Indians—History—Juvenile literature. 2. Pueblo Indians—Social life
and customs—Juvenile literature. [1. Pueblo Indians. 2. Indians of North America—
Southwest, New.] I. Title. II. Series:
    E99.P9R684   1999
    973'.04974—dc21   98-7244
                                                                 CIP
                                                                  AC

Editorial Credits
Timothy W. Larson, editor; Timothy Halldin, cover designer and illustrator;
  Sheri Gosewisch, photo researcher

Photo Credits
Ben Klaffke, 20. Bob Miller, 10. Chuck Place, cover. Dan Polin, 6. John Elk III, 18.
  Noella Ballenger, 16. Photo Network/Bachmann, 8. Valan Photos/John Cancaldsi, 12, 14.

Table of Contents

Map

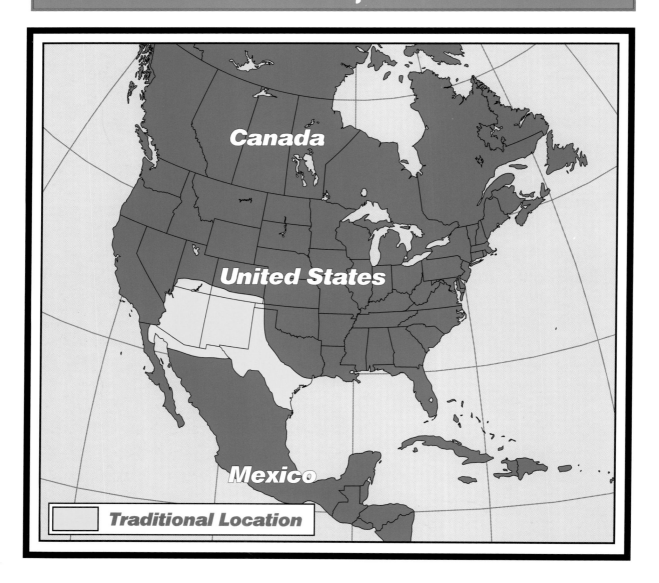

Canada

United States

Mexico

Traditional Location

Fast Facts

These facts tell how the Pueblo Indians once lived. Today, the Pueblos live like most other North Americans. But they also continue to practice valued traditional ways of the past. Some facts about their homes, food, and clothing still are true today.

Homes: The Pueblos lived in box-shaped homes. Some Pueblos built their homes in rows. Others built their homes one on top of another. This building style protected the Pueblos from enemies.

Food: The Pueblos were mainly farmers. At first, corn, squash, and beans were their main crops. Later, the Pueblos also grew peppers and wheat. The Pueblos sometimes ate meat.

Clothing: Pueblo men wore shirts and men's skirts called kilts. Pueblo women wore colorful cotton dresses. Men and women sometimes wore blankets as wraps.

Language: There are four main Pueblo language groups. They are Keresan, Tanoan, Zuni, and Uto-Aztecan.

Traditional Location: The Pueblos' traditional homeland is the southwestern United States. Their homeland lies in a region that covers four states. These states are Colorado, New Mexico, Arizona, and Utah. Some Pueblo groups have lived in parts of Texas and Mexico at times. Today, most Pueblos live in New Mexico and Arizona.

Pueblo History

Long ago, people lived in the area where four states touch today. These states are Arizona, New Mexico, Colorado, and Utah. These people were the Ancient Ones.

The Ancient Ones built villages in cliffs and on mesas. They built these villages between about 200 A.D. and 1300 A.D. The Ancient Ones hunted and gathered food on the mesas. Later they grew food.

The Ancient Ones left their cliff villages by 1300 A.D. Many people believe the Ancient Ones moved because they needed more land and water. They could not grow or hunt enough food on the mesas.

The Ancient Ones moved to the desert floor. They built villages there. They farmed large areas of land. These Ancient Ones became the Pueblo people.

The Ancient Ones left their cliff villages by 1300 A.D.

The Pueblo People

Pueblo means village or village people in the Spanish language. Spanish explorers used this name for the Pueblo in the 1500s. The Pueblo people accepted the name as their own.

The Pueblo Indians live in the southwestern United States. They have lived in villages there for hundreds of years.

Today, most Pueblos live in New Mexico and Arizona. Nineteen Pueblo groups live in New Mexico. These groups include the Acoma, Laguna, Taos, and Zuni. Most of these groups live along the Rio Grande River. The Hopi and the Tewa live in Arizona.

Pueblo communities have their own language and traditions. But they also have some things in common. This book is about the traditions, practices, and history Pueblos share.

Each Pueblo community has its own traditions.

Pueblo Homes

The Pueblo Indians lived in homes in their villages. The homes were box-shaped. Early Pueblos built their homes in cliffs. Later, they built homes on the desert floor.

Pueblos in some villages built single homes in rows. Other Pueblos built their homes in groups. These groups of homes could be four to five houses tall. This saved space and gave Pueblo families shelter from enemies. The Pueblo used ladders to enter their homes.

Pueblos built homes from adobe or sandstone. Adobe is clay. Pueblos formed wet adobe into large blocks. The blocks hardened as they dried in the sun. Pueblos cut sandstone blocks from the ground.

Today, many Pueblo Indians still build traditional-style homes. But they may use modern building materials such as cinder blocks. Pueblos cover these blocks with adobe.

Many Pueblos still build traditional-style homes.

Pueblo Foods

Early Pueblo Indians ate food they hunted and gathered. They gathered plants on mesas. A mesa is the broad, flat land of a cliff top. Pueblos hunted deer on the mesas and in the mountains.

Pueblos later became mainly farmers. They grew crops on the desert floor. The soil there was very dry. But the Pueblos used irrigation to bring water to the soil. They dug ditches that carried river water and rainwater to their fields.

The Pueblo Indians grew many kinds of crops. Corn, beans, and squash were important crops. Later, the Pueblos raised peppers and wheat brought by the Spanish. Many Pueblos still prepare dishes with these vegetables and grains.

Pueblos added other foods to their diet as needed. They gathered berries and nuts. They sometimes ate deer, antelope, or buffalo meat.

Corn is still an important food for the Pueblo.

Pueblo Clothing

The Pueblo Indians used cotton to make most of their clothing. Pueblos grew cotton in fields along with vegetables. Pueblos also used some leather to make clothing.

Pueblo men spun cotton into thread. They used the thread to weave cloth. Weave means to pass threads tightly over and under each other. Many threads make up a piece of cloth.

The Pueblo used the cloth to make clothing. Early Pueblo men wore shirts and kilts. A kilt is a man's skirt. Later, men wore cotton shirts and pants. Pueblo men sometimes still wear traditional clothing.

Pueblo women wore colorful cotton mantas. These dresses wrapped around their bodies and tied at one shoulder. Women wore red belts around their mantas. They sometimes covered their shoulders with blankets. Many Pueblo women and girls wear mantas today.

Many Pueblo women and girls wear mantas today.

15

The Pueblo Family

Family always has been important to the Pueblo Indians. In the past, many family members often lived together as extended families. There were parents, grandparents, and children. Families also could include aunts, uncles, and cousins.

There always was work to do each day. Pueblo family members shared the work. Men and older boys worked in the fields. Women and girls dried foods, ground corn, and cooked meals. Women also took care of young children.

Children learned skills by working with adults. Men taught boys to farm and make tools. They also taught boys how to weave. Women taught girls how to prepare food and make pottery. Men and women taught children how to build homes.

Today, many Pueblo children still learn from adult family members. Adults teach children the traditions of the Pueblo people.

Family has always been important to the Pueblo.

Pueblo Religion

The Pueblo Indians have always had their own religion. Religion is a set of spiritual beliefs people follow. The Pueblo religion taught respect for nature and people. Pueblos understood that nature provided all the things necessary for life. But they also saw that people must work together to live.

The Pueblos believed in kachinas. Kachinas were strong spirits that controlled nature. Pueblos prayed to kachinas for help in their daily lives. They thanked kachinas for their families, homes, and crops.

Pueblo villages had round, underground rooms called kivas. Kivas were the center of Pueblo religious life. Pueblos prayed to kachinas in kivas.

Today, many Pueblo Indians follow the traditional Pueblo religion. Some Pueblos also practice other religions.

Kivas still are the center of Pueblo religious life.

Pueblo Government

Each Pueblo village had a government made up of clan leaders. A clan is a group of family members. Several clans lived together in Pueblo villages.

Clans shared the work of governing a village. Some clans were in charge of village business. Some clans solved village problems. Other clans planned religious events.

Clan members chose leaders. The leaders spoke for clan members. The leaders met as village councils. The village councils met to make important decisions for villages. They also met to make laws and rules.

Today, the Pueblo Indians still have clan governments and councils. Pueblos in some communities vote for council members. The village councils make decisions about laws, finances, and religious events.

Pueblos in some communities vote for their leaders.

Hands on: Make Adobe Bricks

The Pueblo Indians make adobe bricks from clay, sand, straw, and water. They use the bricks to build homes and other buildings. You can make adobe bricks.

What You Need

an adult helper
1/2 gallon (2 liter) bucket
1/4 bucket of modeling clay
1/8 bucket of sand
1/16 bucket of crumbled straw

water
mixing stick
rolling pin
rectangle cookie cutters
wax paper

What You Do

1. Place the clay, sand, and straw in the bucket. Ask an adult to help you mix the ingredients with the mixing stick.
2. Slowly add water to the mixture as the adult stirs. Do not add too much water. The mixture should be like bread dough.
3. Place some of the mixture on a flat surface. Use the rolling pin to flatten the mixture into a thick sheet. The sheet should be about 2 inches (5 centimeters) thick.
4. Use the cookie cutters to cut out your bricks.
5. Place your bricks on the wax paper about one-half inch (1.3 centimeters) apart. Place your bricks outside in the sun to dry. Place your bricks near a sunny window if you live in a wet climate. Turn the bricks over when one side is dry. It may take one week or more for the bricks to dry.
6. Use your adobe bricks to build small houses or buildings.

Words to Know

adobe (uh-DOE-bee)—clay; the Pueblo formed adobe into blocks that dried in the sun.

kachina (kah-CHEE-nah)—a powerful spirit in the Pueblo religion

kiva (KEE-vah)—an underground room used for religious purposes

traditional (truh-DISH-uhn-uhl)—having to do with the ways of the past

Read More

Burby, Liza N. *The Pueblo Indians.* New York: Chelsea House Publishers, 1994.

Fisher, Leonard Everett. *Anasazi.* New York: Atheneum Books for Young Readers, 1997.

Sando, Joe S. *Pueblo Nations: Eight Centuries of Pueblo Indian History.* Santa Fe, N.M.: Clear Light Publishers, 1992.

Sita, Lisa. *Indians of the Southwest: Traditions, History, Legends, and Life.* Philadelphia: Courage Books, 1997.

Useful Addresses

Indian Pueblo Cultural Center
2401 12th Street N.W.
Albuquerque, NM 87104

Mesa Verde National Park
P.O. Box 8
Mesa Verde, CO 81330

Internet Sites

The Hopi Information Network
http://www.InfoMagic.COM/~abyte/hopi/
Indian Pueblo Cultural Center
http://hanksville.phast.umass.edu/defs/independent/
    PCC/PCC.html
Pueblo Indians of New Mexico
http://www.bhs.edu/wmc/lzc/Pueblos.HTML

Index